ENGINES BENEATH US

**ENGINES BENEATH US
MALCOLM DEVLIN**

First published 2020 by TTA Press

ISBN 978-1-9163629-0-1

Copyright © Malcolm Devlin 2020
Copyright © Richard Wagner 2020

The right of the author to be identified as the author of this work has been asserted in accordance with the Copyright, Designs and Patents Act 1988.

All rights reserved. No part of this publication may be reproduced, stored in a retrieval system, or transmitted, in any form or by any means without the prior written permission of the publisher, nor be otherwise circulated in any form of binding or cover other than that in which it is published and without a similar condition being imposed on the subsequent purchaser.

A CIP catalogue record for this book is available from the British Library

Proofread by Peter Tennant

Designed and typeset by the publisher

TTA Press
5 Martins Lane
Witcham
Ely
Cambs CB6 2LB
UK

ttapress.com
shop.ttapress.com

Printed and bound in the UK by 4edge Ltd

FOR HELEN

1

I saw Lee again this morning. He was standing in the doorway of the boarded up butcher's shop opposite the hostel where I'd been living for the past three weeks. I stopped in the reception area, lingering in the shadow of the broken down drinks vending machine, and stared at him through the glass. He hadn't changed at all. A slim, lanky kid in denim and Doc Martens, he was leaning against the doorjamb where the white paint splintered to show the damp and blackened wood beneath. His hands were in his pockets and he wore that familiar expression of aloof contempt as the world passed him by.

I felt light-headed, because in a peculiar way it was such a blessed relief to see him again after so many years, it made me dizzy enough to grab for the vending machine to support myself. But at the same time I was incapable of taking another step forward, fearing my movement would draw his attention. I had no wish for that contempt of his to be directed at me. It would narrow and focus on where I stood like sunlight through a lens and I had no doubt I would burn up under its scrutiny.

We must have stood like that for a good few moments, together and apart, before a cherry-red Fiat Uno pulled up alongside the kerb and I watched him jog down the steps to the passenger door. The driver, a young woman with a bob of bright blonde hair, reached across the seat to unlatch the door, and as he smiled at her I saw that it wasn't Lee after all. The moment passed in a tumbling rush, the boy looked nothing like Lee anymore, and I wondered how I could have imagined he ever might have.

The day resumed as though it had stopped to watch me fooled. It reinstated its normal sense of speed and colour, the sound of traffic and the everyday bustle of the street. The car took off and the empty doorway stared back at me, daring me to blink first, until I took the initiative to move on.

I walked out of the hostel and into the street. There was the threat of rain in the air, the smell of ozone and exhaust fumes. I pulled my collar up higher around my neck and fell in step with the tide of blank-faced strangers on their morning commute, but the kid in the doorway had unanchored me, the Lee-who-was-not-Lee judging the world he perceived had let him down; and so as I walked onwards into the present, my thoughts trailed far behind.

Number 21 had been empty for nearly a year when the Thorel brothers were sent from The Works to clean it up.

It was several weeks before Lee and his da would get there, and with a few other kids from The Crescent, I watched from the road as the Thorels stripped the shutters from the windows and kicked in the door, which had swollen tight in its frame.

They found a colony of mice in the ground floor windows. A rodent city built between the shutters and the glass. It teemed with tiny pink infants; eyes blind to the brightness which had been so rudely revealed to them.

Mick and Dave Thorel were both big, and Mick alone was bigger than most. He had tats and a goatee and enough rings on his fingers he could have punched clean through plate glass. But even he shrieked in surprise when they pried off the metal shutters and he found himself caught beneath a tumbling rain of tiny, panicking creatures. The mice squealed too. The racket woke up the whole street and even Old Elsie turned up to stare, standing across the road, hunchbacked and laden with overstuffed shopping bags.

The Thorels gathered the mice into buckets and took them away. Later, when I asked what had happened to them, Mam said they'd found homes for them all and Da had snorted and told her she was going soft or worse.

Number 21 was in better nick by the time Lee and his da moved in. The window frames had been replaced and the rooms were aired out and given a new coat of paint.

One of the very first things we told Lee when we met him was that the house had been full of mice babies before he moved in.

"The whole ground floor was heaving," we said. "It was full, from floor to ceiling."

We told him about how they had to shovel them into sacks before they could even get into the place. We told him how the little bastards clawed and scratched and bit with hundreds and hundreds of needle teeth.

"A few guys ended up in hospital," we said. "They got completely overrun by the things. They came at them like a wave. They got inside of them. Two of them died."

Lee said we were a bunch of dumb fuck pikey bullshitters.

It took one to know one, his da said.

I turned thirteen that summer and I remember it was a hot one, hotter than I'd remembered it ever being before. The Crescent wasn't built for warm weather; it was a circle of grey rendered semis that soaked up the sun like clay-brick storage heaters, pumping it back at us when the evening looked like it might give us respite. Throughout most of July and August, Da was on night shift, so I wasn't allowed in the house during the day because the heat would keep him awake and the sound of me kicking around would have just wound him up further.

So I spent my days wandering around the neighbourhood or lying on the grass in the middle of The Crescent with a comic or a book. Da was going through a spy novel phase at the time. He had stacks of paperbacks around the house: Fleming, Deighton, le Carré. I'd sometimes grab one I didn't think he'd notice was gone, drawn in by the covers; sex and violence abstracted into silhouettes of nudes and firearms. I guessed I wasn't supposed to be reading them, and when you're that age, the idea that something might be forbidden can make even the dumbest things look awful appealing.

I'd see other kids sometimes. Sid Parry from Number 4 was a lump of a kid but a smart one. He had a buzz cut and an expression that seemed almost permanently bruised. The Bolam twins, Lisa and Nancy, were – to my mind – twins in name only. Lisa was wry and opinionated, black hair cut short so it was harder to pull if she got in a fight; Nancy was quiet and sweet, her freckled face shy behind a tumble of red curls.

There was Craig Peveril too, but he didn't really count. Craig's mam ran The Crescent Neighbourhood Association, which meant they were the ones who lived next door to Mr Olhouser. Craig's mam organised odd jobs for Mr Olhouser and spoke on his behalf when the association met. She wore thin-framed glasses and floral skirts, she tied her hair in a tight bun that yanked her eyebrows up her face so she looked a little bit surprised at everything. But there was steel in the way she sorted out neighbourhood disputes. She organised fundraisers, arranged maintenance crews and just made things work. Mrs Peveril was a formidable sort, but her son wasn't. Craig was thick as shit. He was younger than the rest of us by a few years, but he acted like he was younger still. He was short and impatient; all wound up like a clenched little fist. If it hadn't been for the way his mam would sashay around The Crescent, getting involved in every damn thing that happened, we'd have avoided having anything to do with him at all.

As it was, back then, we didn't really do much. Childhood summers always seem so full of incident until you see them from a distance. We did what kids on the loose usually do when the weather is hot enough to drive them a little crazy.

We ran around, we made shit up, and every day, without exception, we saved the world in time for tea.

We were only doing what every other kid in the city was doing. In every street, on every green, the same games were being played, the same dramas unfolded, but even so, The Crescent had a bit of a reputation back then. It was one of those parts of the city that people were wary of. You probably know the type. It was as though people believed it was the source of everything terrible that happened in the area. You'd sometimes see people stumble in by mistake, only to beat a hasty retreat when we all looked up from what we were doing at the time. I never really understood what they saw: something bleak, something violent, the fulcrum for all the city's ills.

In truth, it wasn't like that at all. In terms of statistics, the neighbouring estates were far worse: assaults, drugs, car theft, murder. Worse: there were whole wars going on between streets out there, if the local news was to be believed. Were anyone to crunch the numbers, they'd notice how no crimes were reported in The Crescent itself. Not that it was all sunshine and light, but The Crescent had its own way of maintaining the law. For the most part, the gangs from the estates kept their distance. Once in a while, one of them would try and make inroads into The Crescent, but they wouldn't get far. They just didn't understand. We had The Works after all, and you didn't mess with The Works, you didn't mess with Mr Olhouser. Not if you wanted the city to keep its head above the water.

You could feel the deep bass thrum of The Works when you were out on the grass, you could feel the distant, buried boom-boom-boom of it when you put your head to your pillow at night. It was always there, and it was ours. That was why we were mostly left to our own devices. We had the city on our side.

But that was something I only really figured out when I was much older. Even at thirteen, our upbringing was sheltered in its way and we were mostly blind to the reputation of our home. That might seem hard to understand, but we didn't really venture outside The Crescent much. In a funny sort of way, it was as though there was a gravitational pull that kept us firmly in our place. But inside, there wasn't much for us to do except pretend we were doing everything else. We'd wander between houses, mucking about, listening to music, watching television or reading the sports pages from the tabloids the guys in The Works sometimes left behind. We'd hang in each other's gardens or amble down the canal, sometimes venturing into the neighbouring estates or following the shipping lines down to the docks, or veering off to the further edges of the more middle class suburbs. It all sounds kind of genteel when put like that, doesn't it? Where were all the drugs and the fighting and the teen promiscuity you see on TV? Well there was some of that as well – we were kids after all – but there was nothing like as much as you might think. Mr Olhouser had very strong opinions about things like that.

There was a sense, I suppose, that our childhood was spent waiting. We were waiting to be old enough for our apprenticeship at The Works to begin, waiting to be introduced to Mr Olhouser when we turned sixteen. And we were impatient as all kids are, never really knowing what we had, just eager to be done with it so we could move on. Always in such a rush, we were. Me and Sid, Lisa and Nancy, Craig running along to catch up. Our futures were all set, only we didn't really know that yet.

Lee was different. Lee came from the outside, not just outside The Crescent, but outside the city itself. He had an accent on him that Lisa swore he was putting on.

There was a swagger to him as well. A cocky confidence, underlined with a cynical air that put years on him. He wore jeans and a bomber jacket; he had big DMs, and he'd clump about the streets with his fists pressed deep into the corners of his pockets.

We all heard things about him: that he'd been kicked out of his last few schools; that the police had a file on him so thick his da had moved them to The Crescent as a last resort to stop him ending up in young offenders.

Lee didn't correct any of the things people said about him but he didn't deny any of it either. He wore the weight of his own notoriety with pride and even my parents were suckered in by the fiction he allowed to extend ahead of him.

"Bad news, that one, Robert," Da said to me one morning. He only used my full name when he thought it might make me listen to him.

He was sitting having his tea while Mam and me were just starting on breakfast.

"Met his old man towards the end of last shift," he said. "Thomas Wrexler, he's called. Tom. Young fella, he is. Worked as a scaffolder up on the north side for the most part, so you'd think he'd know what was what. I was supposed to be showing him the ropes for searing the main catheter. Poor sod is all nerves at the thought of leaving that kid alone each day. Like he's scared he's going to blow the house sky high while he's got his back turned."

He rolled up his sleeve and showed off a mark: a burn, bright and livid from his elbow to mid-way down his forearm. Mam got to her feet to inspect it.

"Where'd you get this?" she said.

"His worry got him careless. He turns round as he's talking and damn near fries my arm off with his iron. All that fretting, so there's something up. Don't worry about it, it's nothing."

He started to roll the sleeve back down but Mam stopped him.

"It'd be nothing if you'd bothered to dress it. For pity's sake, man."

She hurried out of the room and I heard the door under the stairs open and close.

Da watched after her in amusement, then gave me a pointed look.

"Give that kid a wide berth," he said. "He's got trouble all backed up behind him, he only needs miss a step once for it all to come crashing down on him and whoever he's dragged along."

Shortly afterwards, Mam came back with a beaker of tonic, red-grey and thick like milkshake. I could smell it from across the room and recoiled on instinct; it smelled like sour milk and rotten meat.

"Drink this and no fussing," she said.

"Who's fussing?" Da said.

"Just drink it."

He did as he was told. I watched him down the liquid in one, fiercely impressed by the way his face betrayed nothing of the taste of it as he did so. He wiped his mouth with the back of his hand and smiled at Mam.

"And his being from the outside has nothing to do with it," he said. "All outsiders fit in with time. Just…watch your footing with him is all. He doesn't know these roads like you do and I don't want him leading you off the wrong way."

Everyone in The Crescent was employed by The Works to some capacity, and I remember someone saying how the houses of The Crescent were built to house the employees, back when The Works was last renovated in the thirties.

This made some sense of the shape of it. The Crescent was nearly a full circle of identical houses, facing inwards to a central green. The southernmost edge was flattened off. Here, the canal ran from east to west, hidden from The Crescent by a tall brick wall. There was a wide gap in the brickwork that led to the towpath and a narrow, arched footbridge. Boxed in with tall wire fences, the bridge crossed the canal to the back wall of The Works.

The Works was much bigger than it looked, we knew that growing up.

"Like an iceberg," we'd be told, as though we'd ever seen such a thing to compare it to.

Its visible portion squatted beside the canal but the rest of it stretched out deep beneath The Crescent, and from there it extended further still in a tangle of tunnels and corridors and shafts. But that brick wall was all we could see of it until we'd get old enough to be allowed inside.

From The Crescent, The Works looked like a giant, windowless cliff face of red bricks. It blocked off any other view, except for the occasional glimpse of the loading cranes in the docks poking out from above it. I would never describe it as a friendly looking place, but it was solid and reassuring in its own way, a reliable fixed pivot around which the city moved.

When I turned sixteen, my own apprenticeship would begin. Or at least, that was the theory. Mam wasn't keen on the idea. She wanted me to stay in school and maybe go further. She had this crazy idea of me doing a job where I wore a suit and a tie and polished shoes, working somewhere that wouldn't screw with my back, a job that kept normal, regular hours and paid by the month, not the week or the hour. But Mam wasn't really from The Crescent. She'd met Da when they were at school together and they'd married young, much to her parents' consternation. Mam's parents had similar plans for her, they thought she might go on to be a teacher or a nurse, instead she now had a part-time job at the supermarket on the neighbouring estate, which itself was considered eccentric by Mam's friends in The Crescent. She didn't need to work for the outside – no-one else did – but I think she just wanted to keep part of her somewhere else, keep some perspective maybe. Some sort of outlet where she could interact with people who weren't Crescent folk, people who weren't all about The Works, day in, day out. Despite that, she was also part of the Residents' Association and from what I understood she got on well enough with

Mrs Peveril, and they worked pretty well together. But sometimes I got the impression she'd have preferred us to live somewhere else. Like a lot of outsiders she never quite got comfortable with the deep noise of The Works ticking and tocking beneath us. She wore earplugs to sleep, but she could still feel it pounding and pounding and pounding, through the floors, the bed frame, the mattress, like The Princess and the Pea. Da just thought she had funny ideas that she'd brought in from outside. He was Crescent born and bred, as was his father before him; the rhythm of the machinery had been part of him for so long I think he'd have gone crazy if he'd been separated from it. He humoured her but I knew he assumed I'd wind up doing what he did no matter what sort of plans she was making for me.

"The Works got to run," he would say, "or the whole damn city would stop."

He wasn't wrong. Ostensibly, The Works served as the city depot. There'd been a time when everything was handled from there: rubbish collection, road maintenance, signage or changing the bulbs in the street lamps. All those little things which keep a city ticking over came from The Works or went back there at some point. Over the years, a lot of the external jobs had been decentralised by politicians and councillors who didn't really understand what was what. The council now hired contractors to bring in the bins and fix the roads, but The Works was still at the centre of things regardless. They knew how the city really worked and they kept it going day in, day out.

To be absolutely honest, I never did find out exactly what happened in there. Thanks to the events of that summer, my apprenticeship was over before it had begun, but based on the sounds I had grown up with, based on Da's occasional unguarded comments, augmented I'm sure by the stories and comics I read when I was small, I pictured vast underground engines, keeping the city bright and sharp and keen, dwarfing the workers who maintained them.

"We stoke the fires that keep the city working," Da would say, although maybe he read the same stories and comics as I had. He'd been promoted to a shift manager, which got him more pay and longer hours, but I had the sense his work was still rote and repetitive. During his down time at home, he'd devour his books and he'd sing along to the opera he'd record on cassettes from the radio, that big baritone voice of his echoing through the house and upsetting Mrs Clay from next door. He sounded like a starving man gorging on the richest food he could find. If he really was living my future, I sometimes thought, he wasn't doing a good job at selling it back to me.

Assuming I had a choice in the matter, I hadn't made up my mind what I wanted to do. I didn't enjoy school much. All of us Crescent kids went to St Jude's on Bearings Road, a school so threadbare and ill-funded the library was mostly stocked with empty shelves and the maps on the history department's walls were still pink with the bloody fingerprints of faded Empire. Being from The Crescent didn't make things easy there. The other kids were mostly from the surrounding estate and they would avoid or exclude us from all their games and gossip. Even the teachers would act warily, as though we were a pack of grenades primed to go off at any moment.

It was true The Crescent kids seemed a bit scruffier, and on the whole our families seemed less well off in the material sense, but we also looked fitter, a bit ruddier in the cheeks and even having been in fights – and we were always in fights, the other kids in the school made sure of that – we patched up quick and bounced back. No matter what was going around, we never got ill and whatever the circumstances we always showed up. Mr Olhouser was very particular that we should get a good education even if he seemed perfectly happy to cut it off completely once we hit sixteen.

The Crescent had its own lessons, although they were few and far between and their nature was usually frustratingly abstract. I'd been nine or ten the last time and all I really remembered about it was the vague excitement of getting to stay up late on a brisk autumn night. I remember huddling with the other kids outside Lisa and Nancy's place, watching while the adults gathered sombrely on the green. All we could really see were the men from The Works, lined up in a chain around the edge of the grass, their backs turned to us, blocking the view of whatever it was we were supposed to be learning. Between them, we glimpsed fragments of motion like a blurry zoetrope running at half speed. And yet, despite all else, there had been something magical about the night. Something about seeing the whole community together like that stuck with me. If I learned anything, it was that I belonged. I was with my friends, my allies, my people. It was a comforting thought at the time, but even then I caught myself wondering if it was all The Crescent offered us in return.

Because if school was an education in endurance, the alternative didn't seem much better. I didn't want a job in The Works. The idea of spending the rest of my life in The Crescent, working the same shifts Da held now? Even then, that didn't sound enough to me. Maybe it was true that Mam's aspirations for me had gone to my head, or maybe there was just some of her restlessness that had grown in me unattended. Either way, staying put felt like treading water when I could have been striking out for the horizon.

So maybe I was looking for a way out all along. Lee Wrexler was from the outside. Maybe that was enough.

2

To begin with, I did as I'd been told and steered clear of Lee as best as I could. But again, when you're young and you're told not to do something, it becomes fascinating in a way that can override common sense.

And besides, it was Lee who came to talk to me. Not the other way around.

I was on my back in the middle of The Crescent with a copy of *2000AD* I'd stolen from Sid's collection. It was an old copy and I must have read it a dozen times. Kreelman was framing Johnny Alpha for murder, just as he did every other time I read it. Sid didn't have the next few issues, but there were a few more recent editions kicking around, so I knew he wouldn't get away with it.

A shadow fell across me and I saw Lee's now familiar shape, hands in pockets, staring down.

"What's that you've got, then?" he said.

"Comic."

"No shit. Let me see."

He took it from me, before I could reply and inspected it. "This is ancient," he said. "You not got anything newer?"

I shook my head.

He turned it over in his hands as though he was trying to decide what to do with it. Then he looked down at me and shook his head as though I was simple and he was sympathetic.

"So let's go get you some new ones," he said.

I don't know what I'd been expecting. I probably thought he had a stash of comics somewhere. Maybe stacked up in his room up at Number 21, or maybe tucked away somewhere else, down in a lockup off the canal path. For some reason, he struck me as the sort of kid who would hide things in places.

It was a bit of a disappointment when he led me to a comic book shop instead. It might have been the obvious place to go, but it seemed prosaic, a bit ordinary, and it certainly didn't fit the complex mystique the other kids and I had engineered for him.

We didn't really talk much on the bus ride there. Lee had Sid's comic folded in front of him but his thoughts were clearly elsewhere. I kept casting him glances to see if he'd forgotten I was there. I didn't want to say anything in case I put him off, so I just stared out of the window at the city I barely knew, catching his pensive reflection jitter in the window whenever the bus ran under a bridge.

There were only two things that would make me go into the city proper.

Mam would take me to visit Grandma sometimes; she lived in a nursing home by the river and on sunny days we'd walk down the canal until we got to the locks near the city centre. We didn't really do much when we got there but Mam said Grandma just liked us being there with her. Grandma didn't really say a lot those days. She moved slowly like she was underwater. But she liked her jigsaws so we'd spend hours silently finding edge pieces for her.

The other occasion we would go into town was when the fair was on, and over that weekend, a gang of us would take the bus and just troll around the rides, trying to pick the scariest looking thing to spend our handful of change on. There was sometimes a bit of tension between us from The Crescent and the guys who ran the fair; there was always something a bit standoffish about them and you could see their expressions sharpen when they picked us out of the crowd. Usually, there'd be a fight somewhere that'd make the local news, but no-one really got hurt and Da insisted it was only good natured rivalry in the end: like we had more in common with them than with the rest of the city and the lads from the fair knew it well enough.

I'd never been to the shop Lee led me to. It was called Cosmix and it was a small place on the outskirts of the central district. It had a brightly appointed sign and a crowded display window, but inside was gloomy with only a dull amber light distorting the colourful panels displayed along the walls.

Behind the counter, a thin young man in round spectacles tensed when the bell above the door signalled our arrival. The atmosphere was a bit close, a bit warm, but once my eyes had adjusted to the light, the boxes of books and comics were like the lure on the end of a fishing line.

Lee and I separated, allowing ourselves to be led to different parts of the shop. When I reached deep into the boxes it was like I was finding treasure with every handful I brought up.

I found myself reading *Swamp Thing*. I don't know why I picked it up, but it didn't take me long before I got caught up in it. I must have got through a handful of copies before the guy at the counter cleared his throat.

"You gonna buy that?"

"What?"

"You going to buy that? This is a shop, not a library. I've got to sell these."

He came round the counter and started packing away the issues I'd already read. I hadn't even been aware that I was making a mess, but he fussed over the discarded issues as he set them back where they belonged.

I bristled.

"I'm just looking."

"You've been looking for the best part of an hour."

And then Lee was beside me, all insolence and charm.

"Well maybe if you had a better selection," he said, "he'd find something worth buying."

The man's face whitened, his lips puckered like he was going to spit at us.

Instead, he marched around the back of the counter and picked up the telephone.

Without looking, Lee plucked up one of the *Swamp Thing* comics I'd been looking at and slapped it on the counter. The man stared at it like he wasn't sure whose side the comic was on.

Lee smiled. A friendly, we're-all-mates-here sort of smile. He fished out his wallet and opened it to reveal a pair of notes.

"Come on," he said. "Your customers are getting restless."

I don't think I breathed until we were back outside again. Lee passed me the bag with the comic he'd bought in it.

"Congratulations," he said. "It's not a new one, to be honest, but it's a bit more up to date than the shit you were reading before."

He swung around and sauntered down the street, pausing at the corner for me to catch up.

"Besides which," he said, opening his jacket, "this lot is fresh."

A stack of comics dropped from under his coat and fanned out at our feet. *Daredevil*, *Hellblazer*, *Batman*, more. Their colours were vivid in the early afternoon sun.

I confess, I gaped at him.

"But he was staring at you the whole time!" I said. "He never took his eyes off you."

Lee stooped to pick up his hoard; he passed them to me and gestured to the bag he'd given me earlier. I slipped them inside and they felt fat and heavy and expensive.

"He barely saw me," Lee said. "He was looking at you. You're a Crescent kid. Hate to be the one to break it to you, but people can spot you a mile off. You should have seen the way he looked at you."

He slapped me on the back and smirked.

"You're a useful guy to have around," he said.

That was the beginning of my short-lived life of crime. After our raid on Cosmix, we used the same trick on other shops around the area. We started with other comic book stores, before progressing to bookshops, record shops, supermarkets and off-licences. And you know what? It was so easy. I'm not being cocky, I didn't have to do anything other than look like I came from The Crescent and that was more than enough. I just stood near the counter and drew the staff's attention, while Lee cleaned up elsewhere.

We started refining our act. I'd dress down; I'd borrow one of Da's old donkey jackets and muss up my hair until I looked like something out of a Dickens novel. Lee would hang about outside and come in later so it wouldn't look like we were there together.

We never took much, but we took more than we could have afforded to actually buy. We'd divvy up our takings around the corner from the shops and when I got home I'd stash them in a box under my bed. CDs I had no means of playing, bottles of beer I couldn't imagine ever drinking, books I couldn't imagine reading. It was never really about what we took, and instead I began to consider it some kind of payback, and the exhilaration of it bred a sense of punch-drunk entitlement. I'd think of the way the shopkeepers had looked at me, that look of wary distaste when they saw who'd come in.

Look at me like that, I thought, and you deserve everything you get.

Sometimes I went round Lee's house although I found it a little bleak. The furniture was threadbare and didn't match, like it had been pieced together from house sales and charity shops, and the rooms stank of lingering cigarette smoke. The kitchen was mostly bare, with stacks of tins and multipack super noodles. Lee's da didn't cook, and Lee certainly wasn't interested in learning.

I'd see Lee's da sometimes. He'd sit in the lounge watching football on a small TV set, the volume turned up high to mask the distant whomp-whomp-whomp of The Works underneath. He was a tall, slim man, a scrappy beard filling in the pits in his cheeks that had been worn down by worry. He was younger than my da, but his eyes seemed older. He would look at me, then through me, then past me. He would smile sometimes, but it was a delicate thread of an expression, too easily snapped and washed away.

He didn't really talk to us, not even the usual parent-speak formulae designed to steer us to a more reliable path. He'd just nod in acknowledgement that we were there, and then drift off again into his own little world.

There was one time I remember when he spoke to me properly. Lee had left me in the kitchen while he went off to get something from upstairs and Lee's da came in. I don't think he realised I was in the house and I remember him hesitating in the doorway as though deciding whether or not to come in. There was that slightly awkward tension you sometimes get when two people who don't really know what to say to each other are left alone to make conversation.

"So you've always lived here?" he said.

It sounded like one of those nothing questions you get from people who don't know what to say, but I remember he looked at me intently as though the answer really was important to him.

"Yes," I said, "over there." I gestured vaguely to where our house was but he looked oddly saddened.

"Funny isn't it?" he said. "How one person's last resort is all some other poor sod will ever know?" And he smiled this strange, sad smile that I couldn't quite get a handle on.

Lee appeared behind him then, pulling on his coat and gesturing for me to leave. Lee's da stepped out of my way and avoided my eyes as I passed him. I think that must have been the last time he ever spoke to me. Apart from at the lesson, of course.

Lee never really spoke about his da at all. He didn't speak of his mam either, but I saw at least one photograph of the three of them propped by his bed one time I went round, small and faded in too big a frame. She looked ordinary, kind, and the little Lee in her arms was beaming in a way I couldn't imagine the Lee I knew to smile. I didn't say anything, but he caught me looking at it and it wasn't there the next time I went round.

Sometimes he would relate anecdotes about his life before The Crescent. They were few and far between, often coming out of nowhere, like they'd been bubbling up inside of him, and would have burst out of him had he not had an outlet.

"We had a proper garden in the last place we lived in," he said once. We were standing in the back of Number 21, a sheltered wedge of dried grass and moss dwarfed by the surrounding walls. "I mean, neither me or dad ever did any gardening or anything, so it just went wild. Only there it really did go wild. Grass up to here. Dandelions, thistles.

"Anyway, one day, I was out there, you know." He mimed

a gesture like he was smoking. "And I see something in the grass at the back of the garden that I'd never seen before. And it's under this plant. Pink. Lilac, that's what it was, a lilac. And under it there was this dog, a collie, like one of those sheepdogs, you know? I don't know how it got in, but there it was."

"Did you keep it?" People didn't really have pets in The Crescent, so I might have sounded keener than I intended.

Lee shook his head. "Nah," he said. "Poor mutt was dead."

I spluttered in surprise, but Lee shot me a serious look.

"There was a name on the collar," he said. "Turns out it was owned by the people who used to live in the house and the dog used to spend its summers lying under this lilac bush. Dad called them. They said how much she loved that garden. And so, when her time came, when she was good and ready, she found her way home."

"What did you do?" I said, suspicious the story was still due to take a transgressive turn.

But Lee only shrugged, losing interest.

"We buried her, of course," he said.

Usually, he would just let me talk, twittering excitedly about the things we'd done, listening with an amused tolerance, like someone older than he was. But I don't think it was enough for Lee. He was humouring me with easy pickings, but I knew The Crescent bored him, made him restless, and I should have known that our tiny, nascent criminal empire wouldn't have held his attention for long.

"Oh man," Lee said one day. "Will you look at the state of her?"

We were by the canal, opposite the back wall of The Works. We'd been wasting time, throwing stones and sticks into the water, and I'd been talking about how Da had promised he was going to take me fishing up at the Hollow. Lee had been only barely interested, distracted by the shadows of crayfish he could see picking their way across the bottom of the canal like articulated tanks. Now he was staring down the towpath.

I looked up to follow his finger and saw that Old Elsie was standing further up the canal path, staring blankly into the water. She was outside the tall wooden gate that led into the garden of Number 17 where Mr Olhouser lived. It was covered with a heavy iron grill, bolted to the wall on all sides. I'd never seen it open. I'd never seen it unlocked.

I said her name and Lee shot me a look.

"You know her? Jesus, Rob, you hang with some real freaks, you know that?"

I shrugged and sat down on the bank of the canal, waving my feet over the edge. My reflection stared back. I imagined it crawling with fat crayfish.

"Everyone knows her," I said. "She's always been here."

I glanced up, checking her distance. Old Elsie looked like a homeless woman but she wasn't really, not anymore. She was old and weathered, her back curved and her shoulders hunched. She carried handfuls of carrier bags, stuffed with rubbish and things she just found lying around that she must have thought were interesting. She never looked at anyone. I don't think anyone really looked at her. She was just there.

But Lee was looking.

"Shit," he said. "She looks rough. Do you see her chin? She's got a fucking beard on her!"

I thought he was being too loud. I glanced around, conscious that we might be overheard. But Old Elsie didn't move and I wondered if she could hear anything at all.

"I guess she was homeless," I said, my voice much quieter as though it might steer him into lowering his own.

"Yeah, but still," he said. "We should do a whip round, get her a Ladyshave."

He snapped a stem of grass from the bank and sat down beside me, flicking the surface of the water with the grass and sending our reflections eddying apart. His grin faltered when he saw the way I was staring at him.

"The fuck I say now?" he said.

"Don't go near her," I said. "I mean it."

He laughed at that but his expression was puzzled.

"What? Are you jealous?" he said.

I looked at him like he was an idiot.

"No way, it's just—"

"'Keep your hands off my bag lady'?"

"Fuck off," I said. "She's Mr Olhouser's."

He blinked.

"You what?" he said.

I stood up and took a step away. I had never liked saying Mr Olhouser's name out loud, certainly not so close to where he lived. Even said at a whisper from a safe distance, I'd always thought it sounded too loud and obvious, like it sucked in attention from places you didn't want attention from.

Ahead of us, up the path, Old Elsie had turned to face us. I hadn't seen her move, but then I never saw her move.

"Just…keep away from her," I said. "And the others. Keep away from them too. I'm serious. I'm really serious."

Lee stumbled to his feet. He tossed the strand of grass behind him and stared at me.

"I don't know what the fuck you're talking about," he said. "Has this Olhouser got some harem of bag ladies or something?"

I shook my head, it all felt backwards. The idea that Lee didn't know made no sense to me. It was something that I'd always known. It was like knowing that nettles will sting you, the oven will burn you, cars can kill you if you don't pay attention. Little day-to-day instructions you learn young which stop you hurting, stop you getting killed.

If they belong to Mr Olhouser, we learned, you leave them alone; you stay well away.

And yet Lee was staring at me like I was the crazy one, and at that moment I felt as though there was nothing I could say to him. I got up and walked away.

I should have told him. The whole exchange should have tipped me off that he didn't know how things worked in The Crescent and I should have taken it as my cue to sit down and tell him everything. He would never have believed a word, he would have laughed in my face, but I should have told him anyway.

Da called them indentured. I didn't really know what that meant and I was far too self-conscious to ask.

Around that time, there were three of them I knew of. Old Elsie was the one I saw most, but there was also The Priest, who was a tall thin figure in a threadbare cassock.

He would stand in the shadows of buildings, wavering like a reed in the riverbed. The third we called Copper; he was a red-haired figure who looked like he might have once been a policeman. He would stand motionless in open spaces, his hands alternatively raised and outstretched as though he were conducting the traffic at rush hour.

From a distance they looked like normal people, but the closer you got the air around them seemed to thrum with something discordant. And if you got too close, you might see that their faces were slack and their eyes were hollow pits.

There had been others I remembered seeing from when I had been younger. The Broker, The Clown, The SadAndLonelyMother, but I hadn't seen any of them for some time, certainly not since the lesson we'd had put on for us when I'd been nine, when they'd stood silently together in the middle of the green, staring blankly into space. Since then, it was as though they'd just faded away, and until I met Lee it honestly didn't occur to me that they might be strange to anyone else.

So it shouldn't have surprised me that Lee would be curious. As I've said already, any instruction not to do something would only incite me to do the opposite, so I'd have undoubtedly done the same if I had been him. But I'd been brought up to keep away from Mr Olhouser until the day he wanted to see me after I'd started my apprenticeship. I'd been brought up to keep away from his people like you keep your distance from wasps and bees, like you don't walk out in front of cars, how you don't slam your foot in the door, how you don't stick your hand under the hot tap because it'll just get hotter still.

When I walked away from Lee that day, I honestly believed I'd said enough, that the subject would be dropped and we could just get on with the summer as though it hadn't been mentioned at all.

Weeks passed lazily. Da came off night shift and we got used to seeing more of him again, sitting at the breakfast table in his overalls, reading his paper, drinking his mug of tea like he always had.

I'd still get out of the house during the day, and when Lee was busy with other things, which happened more and more as the summer waned, I'd catch up with Sid and the Bolam twins, amongst whom my friendship with Lee had not gone unnoticed.

"My da told me to keep clear of him," Sid said.

We were in the garden behind the Bolams' house, a narrow quadrangle of fusty grass and moss that the twins' parents made only minimal effort to tend. Sid had some of his older comics laid out before him. He was folding pages, pleating the paper so the people in them looked distorted; shrunken or broken in grotesque ways, like their legs were splayed at unnatural angles.

"Ours and all," Lisa said. She was sitting against the fence, teasing apart the yellow bud of a daisy she had picked. She looked up at me, eyes narrow. "He steals things," she said.

I couldn't deny that one, so I kept quiet. It struck me as a bit unfair though. They'd each taken a turn to read the comics Lee and I had lifted, and they'd been excited to do so at the time. As far as I was concerned, they were as complicit in the crime as Lee or I was.

But Lisa wasn't done.

"You know he killed his mam, right?" she said.

"He didn't kill his mam."

"Did too. Heard so from Craig. He said Lee gets so angry he sees nothing but red, and even when he was little he got all mad and jumped at her while she was driving and she crashed her car."

Nancy nodded but didn't say anything. She was trying to make a daisy chain but the materials were letting her down. A pile of broken flowers was mounting beside her, stems torn, petals scattering.

"Craig said he's got scars all over him from the crash," Lisa said. She traced a hand over her chest and stomach. "All over. There was glass and blood everywhere. And when the ambulance came, they found them both covered in blood and there he was, just sitting on her chest like a demon."

I rolled my eyes.

"Bullshit," I said. "He wasn't even in the car."

I hadn't known Lee for long before he dismantled the myths I'd heard. It was true he'd moved from school to school, but that was because his da was unlucky with work. They'd kept moving from town to town to try and get yet another fresh start, yet another break. He had no criminal record, not so far anyway. And during the height of a snowstorm, his mother had lost control of her Citroen 2cv. It had swerved into the path of an oncoming eighteen-wheeler while Lee, aged four at the time, had been at his grandmother's house, waiting for her to come home.

Lisa shrugged.

"Well," she said. "Who you going to believe?"

Not Craig, that was for sure. Craig was a needy little kid, who would resort to being gross because he thought it might impress us. It got him an audience sometimes, but I doubt it was the sort of thing his mam would have been pleased to hear about.

Nancy unfolded her daisy chain, only six links, but the breeze took it and carried it high like a pendant. She smiled at her success.

"Anyway," her sister said, "I hear he's been bothering Old Elsie."

"Craig tell you that, too?"

"We saw him. Nancy and me, both," she said. "He was just hanging around near her, watching her."

I didn't like the sound of that, but the weird thing was that I don't think I was scared for him then. I'd warned him well enough, so I thought he wouldn't push things too far. Instead, I think I was hurt he hadn't told me what he was doing. I was hurt he'd left me out of his game.

"I'll talk to him," I said.

Lisa laughed.

"Yeah, right," she said. "Like he'd care."

"Course he will," I said. "He's not an idiot."

But I didn't see Lee for the next couple of days. I was going to, really I was, but we got news that my grandma had taken ill and so everything got thrown out of order.

Grandma's heart had been teetering on the brink of giving out for the past year or so. This time, she'd been taken to the hospital in the city and we all spent the next few days lingering around the ward, waiting for something conclusive to happen.

Mam brought a flask of tonic for her, but it had turned black once she was out The Crescent and smelled even more awful than normal. She just left it in her bag, then threw the whole flask away when she got home rather than try and clean it out.

Grandma lay on the bed like a tiny doll, the thin covers pushed aside like they were all too heavy for her. When she smiled at us, she looked so apologetic, as though the whole thing was this awkward inconvenience she never meant to put us all through. She died late on the Thursday night, and it was one of those things that even though you saw it coming from a long way off, none of us could step out of its way, so the force of it hit us full on regardless.

The next few days were heavy with the ritual and observances of mourning. Tears and paperwork and sombre meetings with soft-spoken gentlemen in charcoal grey suits. The Crescent gathered around us. Grandma wasn't from The Crescent, but in this case that didn't matter. The Crescent looked after its own, and we found ourselves at the centre of a community falling over itself to lend us support. The wake went on until long into the following morning, and if Mrs Peveril hadn't started ushering people home when she saw just how tired we all were, it would probably have gone on much longer. Even when it was all over and done, we'd been given so many plates of food we had to start throwing them out before they turned.

So Lee and Old Elsie completely slipped my mind.

A week or so later, it was Lee who came to see me instead. Only he came at three in the morning and he hammered on the door of the house, screaming my name.

⊕

I'd been asleep of course, and the noise Lee made broke into my dreams and tore them down around me. I stared at the ceiling in my room, lit a dull orange by the halogen light from the street outside. I waited until I was sure I was awake; until I could figure out if the noises I could hear were real or not.

There were voices downstairs. Lee's was the loudest, inflected with a note of panic that made me doubt it was really him at all, but I could hear my parents too, more hushed, more subdued, trying their best to quieten him down before Mrs Clay from next door started banging on the walls again.

I picked my way downstairs to find them all in the hallway by the front door. Mam was in her dressing gown; Da was wearing the vest and tracksuit pants he used as pyjamas. He was holding Lee like he'd been wrestling with him. His big forearm hooked around Lee's skinny stomach, blocking the kid's arms from moving. But Lee was wriggling and fidgeting. He looked terrible. His eyes were wide and crazy, his face was streaked with dirt and his jacket was torn; there was blood along his forearm to the heel of his hand.

When he saw me on the stairs, he seemed to snap into focus.

"Rob!" he said. "We've got to get out of here. We've all got to get out of here. This place... This fucking place..."

He struggled to find an adequate expression to complete the thought, but faltered. I'm ashamed to admit I just froze on the stairs, staring at him. I'd only known him for what amounted to weeks, a month or two at best, but I'd never seen him frightened before. He wasn't shocked-frightened like you get when you hear a sudden loud noise; he wasn't worried-frightened either, like Mam was when she heard how Grandma was ill. Lee was terrified. Like his world had been ripped out from under him and he'd been left flailing in the blackness it left behind. He'd been cast loose into nothingness, and there was Da trying to hold him down and stop him drifting away.

Mam fussed over him.

"Where's your dad?" she said.

Da grunted and answered for him. "He's on nights this week," he said.

"So there's no-one home?"

"What happened?" I said. "What's going on?"

"We've got to go," Lee said. "You've got to get my dad, they won't let me into The Works, I banged on the door but they wouldn't let me inside."

"Jesus," Da said.

Mam shot me a look, as though she thought I might know what was going on, then she turned back to Lee.

"Let's get you into the kitchen," she said, her voice soft and friendly like she was talking to a five-year-old. "You can tell us all about it and I can take a look at that arm of yours. Deal?"

Lee's head bobbed with consent. I don't think he really heard what she said but he visibly relaxed at the tone of her voice. Da lifted his hands away slowly and let Mam steer Lee into the kitchen.

Da glanced up at me, standing uselessly on the stairs. The stark lighting in the hallway accentuating his look of concern.

"Maybe you should go back to bed," he said. "Your mam and me can take care of this."

Mam's voice called from the kitchen.

"Let him stay. He'll calm the boy," she said.

Da didn't argue. He stepped aside and let me pass, stooping to pull his work boots on over his bare feet.

"He'll be alright," he said to me. He didn't say anything else. He didn't ask me why Lee had come to our house when Da had told me to keep away from him. He just reached for his overcoat and shrugged it on.

Lee was sitting at the kitchen table, his hands out before him, the wound on his arm bleeding slowly, pooling on the wooden surface.

"I'm going to have to cut your jacket," Mam said. "Robbie, the orange-handled scissors are in the top drawer over there."

I retrieved them and handed them to her.

"What happened?" I said again.

Mam looked helpless. She looked past me to where Da stood in the doorway.

"What happened, son?" Da said, his voice quiet.

Lee looked up, but he didn't look at Da, he stared at me as though I was the only one in the room with him, as though I might be the only one capable of understanding him.

"I only wanted to see," he said.

"What did you see?"

He looked down at the table. Maybe it was the way Mam was talking to him, but he suddenly seemed much younger than he had been before. All those layers of pretence he wore were shucked away, leaving him raw and exposed. He stared wide-eyed at the slow progress of the blood on the tabletop. It extended in long fingers of rich crimson along the grain.

"The bag lady," he said, his voice small. "I followed her. I wanted to see."

"The bag lady?" Mam looked up.

"Old Elsie," I said.

Da shook his head.

"Jesus," he said again. "I'll go fetch his old man. Keep him here. Don't let him go anywhere."

He ducked out of sight quickly, like he would have taken any excuse to leave. We heard the front door slam behind him.

Calmly and patiently, Mam set the scissors to the sleeve of Lee's denim jacket and began slicing up his arm.

"Why don't you tell us what happened?" she said.

Lee swallowed hard, his eyes fixed on the table in front of him.

"I wanted to know where she came from," he said. "I know Rob said to leave her be, but…I don't know. She just didn't make any sense."

He looked up at me, begging to be understood.

"Because you've seen her, right?" he said. "One moment she's in one street and the next she's in another, but if you try and figure out where she goes in a day, it doesn't seem to work like that. She shouldn't be able to get from The Crescent to the North High Street quicker than it takes you to get a bus, but she does. It's always like she's there waiting for you.

"So I followed her." He shrugged. "Well, I say I followed her, she barely moves. Not while you pay any attention to her. So I just waited around nearby, looking at my watch, reading a paperback, looking somewhere else or something."

He shot me a glance at that; it was odd to think that the same boy had been so confidently teaching me how to lift comics only a few weeks earlier.

"And when you're not really looking at her, she's off on her way. And she never moves fast. But if you want to follow her, you've got to be both slow and quick. Slow, because she takes her time, but quick because once she's turned the corner? You've lost her. It's like she just lifts up her skirts and takes off like a rocket. She's just gone when you get there yourself.

"So I kept an eye out, you know? I waited and watched, and when I saw she was on the move, I'd figure out where she might be going and I'd go ahead to the street she might be turning down and I'd wait there. Anyway, I lost her a few times doing that but today..."

Mam peeled back the sleeve of Lee's jacket. There was a wide, angry looking cut running from his shoulder down the length of his bicep. The bleeding appeared to have slowed, but the blood upon it was jewel-bright.

Mam filled a bowl of water at the sink and set it on the table, she looked up at me.

"Robbie, can you get the first aid box for me," she said. "It's in the bathroom cupboard, at the back."

"But I want to hear!"

"Then you'd better be quick then."

I took the stairs two at a time. The bright fluorescence of the bathroom light made my eyes sting as I searched through the cupboard until I found the green plastic first aid box. It had been there since I could remember, and when I was younger it was like a mouldering treasure chest. Full of interesting looking things, individually wrapped and yellowing with age, but we never really seemed to use anything from it at all.

I killed the bathroom light and ducked back onto the landing, the box wedged tightly under my arm. The landing light bulb had blown earlier in the week and no-one had got round to replacing it, so the only light came from the streetlight outside, and my eye was drawn to the figure standing beneath it. Old Elsie faced away from me, her head slightly bowed, her bags heavy in each hand.

I hung by the window for a moment, foolishly imagining I might see her move in a way Lee had said she never did, but she was silent and still and I wondered how long she had been waiting out there. Had Da seen her when he went out? Wouldn't he have said something if he had? It was such a strange, disorientating thing. Old Elsie had never bothered me before. None of them had. They'd just been there and I'd known well enough to keep my distance.

In the kitchen, Lee was still talking. He still seemed to be addressing the space I'd left behind. Mam took the first aid box from me and opened it. She'd already washed the cut on Lee's arm and began to dress it with wadding and a bandage. She watched me while she did it. She gave me this long look, locked in neutral, like this whole thing was some obscure sort of lesson she'd arranged herself.

"She just stands there, in the garden, waiting," Lee said. "And it took me a while to realise she was waiting for me to just fuck off – excuse me – to go away and leave her be."

His eyes found me again and they sharpened.

"Have you seen the garden there?"

I shook my head.

"At Number 17? I went inside to see. Looking for dogs, you know." He risked a smile, but it flickered and fell. "I jumped over the gate near the canal, because she was standing outside it one moment and then she was inside. I swear the gate didn't open but in she goes. So I climb up the iron grill to the top of the wall, and over the other side, there are all these stumps of tree trunks in there. It's not a big garden and it's all boxed in by these big walls on every side and the house on the other, but there are these tree stumps all lined up like football players, you know. It's like they're in four-four-two formation give or take. Only it doesn't make sense really. Because you'd never get trees growing that close to each other. Never so they'd grow that big. They're about this high."

He held his hand up about four foot from the kitchen floor.

"So she's there in the middle waiting for me. And so I jump down off the top of the wall, and I just stood there on the other side of that gate, waiting for her to do something else. It was like we were playing chicken with each other, seeing who was going to blink first."

He sighed and looked at Mam.

"Can I have something to drink please?"

"Robbie."

I grabbed a mug from the cupboard and filled it at the sink. Lee drank greedily, then held it back out to me expectantly. I refilled it and left it on the table in front of him.

"So I gave up. I didn't want to, but I couldn't stay in that garden. It's crazy, she's just this little old lady, but it felt so wrong there. Like the actual place didn't want me to be there. I felt sick. Properly, physically sick. It was so warm, but heavy warm. Humid, you know. And there was no other way out. The house was dark, all the windows were just black you know. No curtains, just black like it was empty. But there was no way through without breaking in and I wasn't going to do that. Only way out was back the way I'd come, so I turned my back on her."

He took another drink of the water.

"It's a big wall. On the canal side, there's those mooring posts you can stand on to get a bit of height. And there's the grill on the gate you can find footholds in, but inside? There's none of that. It's just this wall going up and the gate? There's nothing on it. Wooden planks, no handle, no catch. Nothing. It's locked from the outside, Rob. From the outside.

"Anyway, there I am thinking I'll never get over this bloody thing. I'm stuck here. I'm stuck here with her."

He paused.

"And then I hear this noise behind me. This creaking, crackling, flapping noise. Like someone folding up a wet tarpaulin. Only it's not just behind me, it's all around me and it's getting louder and louder. It's getting closer. And there's this smell. God, that smell! Like the canal when it all gets backed up and doesn't move for a month..."

He laughed.

"Holy shit – sorry. I have no idea how I did it, but that gets me up the wall. This noise kicks up, this smell and suddenly I'm a fucking Ninja. I'm Spiderman. I was up that wall quick as you can imagine. There's some broken glass up on the top, not a lot but enough so I rip my arm open when I'm doing it, it hurt like almighty fuck – I'm sorry – it hurt. But still...

"And my heart is pumping like crazy, but I'm high on adrenaline and I'm sitting on top of this wall and you know, all things considered I'm feeling a bit smug about myself. And then I look back. I look down. And Elsie's gone. She's not there at all. But those tree stumps? They've moved. They're not in the middle of the garden anymore, they're all bunched up at the bottom of the wall. Just where I was standing."

Mam rolled down what was left of his sleeve. Lee's hand was shaking.

"Wait here," she said. "I'm going to get you a glass of tonic. It'll help with the healing."

Lee didn't react. Mam got up and went into the hall. I heard the door under the stairs open, then bang shut, and footsteps clump down to the basement.

"You're an idiot," I said when I was sure she was out of earshot. "You don't know how lucky you are."

Lee shook his head.

"You haven't heard the best part," he said. "She followed me."

"Old Elsie?"

Lee nodded.

"I went home. Who am I kidding? I ran home. Faster than I've ever ran. But I thought it was over, you know. It didn't occur to me she would have a mind to follow me, I just wanted to be home quick as I could. But the house...it felt wrong. I mean it was never cosy, but it was just too dark and too empty and too cold. I go upstairs to the bathroom to take a look at my arm, but when I get to the landing? I see her through the window. She's outside my fucking house. She's under the streetlight and I swear to you, she's standing there like she wants me to see her."

I stared at him, a cold, dead weight calcifying in my gut.

"What happened?"

"I ran downstairs and opened the door. I know, I know. It sounds stupid. I mean why would you do something like that? But I was angry. I was furious. This was my place. I'd gone home, the game was over. And I wanted to give her an earful or…I don't know, I hadn't really thought it through. Anyway, I open the door and she's not there anymore. The street's completely empty.

"I don't leave the doorway. I'm not a complete idiot. I just look outside, and she's gone. Really, she's gone. So I close the door and I go back in. I close the door. I check all the locks, you know…

"And I'm standing in the hallway, trying to figure out what to do next, when there's that noise again. This crackling, creaking, snapping noise. And there's this smell. This smell like rotting vegetables, stagnant water…

"And behind that glass on the basement door, this shape has started…growing. Like a shadow learning how to stand up on its own. And it's all twisted and dark and… And then something reaches forward and bangs at the glass like it wants in.

"And that's when I run. That's when I unlock the front door and run. That's when I run to The Works. That's when I run here."

But by that point, I was almost running myself. I bundled into the hall and fumbled with the latch on the front door. I could hear Lee pushing back his chair to follow me as I opened the door and ran onto the pathway outside and into the street.

There was no-one under the streetlight, The Crescent was empty, like a curfew had been imposed. A circle of orange streetlights against a velvet blue black sky; the thin white halo which surrounded The Works. The street was still and Old Elsie had gone.

I ducked back inside, slamming the door behind me and checking the catch.

"What is it?" Lee said.

Breathless, I told him how I'd seen Old Elsie before when I went upstairs and it felt horribly wrong describing back to him what he'd only just described to me.

"Why didn't you say something?"

His voice was hoarse.

"Because she's never meant anything before," I said. "She never did anything until you started following her around."

He looked like I'd punched him, and for a moment I could have. His face had slackened, that contemptuous self-righteousness of his stripped away and leaving him looking doughy and foolish. He'd never seen me angry before and he stepped away from me like all those kids in St Jude's who lived in fear of The Crescent kids and gave us a wider berth than we deserved. Roughly, I pushed past him and his balance teetered. He watched dumbly as I set my hand on the basement door handle, and my palm was already laced with sweat.

"What are you doing?" Lee was flapping. "We've got to go. We've got to go now. Where's your mum gone?"

"She's in the basement." My voice was flat.

Lee swallowed hard.

"Rob," he said.

"Shut up."

I took a breath then opened the door. An empty space glowered back; the stairs wound downwards into an amber gloom, the insistent pulse of distant machinery rising like a heartbeat.

"Wait here," I said. I plunged inside.

I don't know what I was expecting. The basement looked as it always did. It was a low ceilinged chamber roughly the size of the kitchen. The walls were uneven and slightly damp, as though the room had been carved from the stone foundations and had yet to be properly domesticated. A series of metal pillars like scaffolding poles were positioned at intervals, holding up the floorboards above.

Half of the room was stuffed with boxes, the other half was the dispensary, both were lit by a pair of whining fluorescent tubes dividing the ceiling.

There was no sign of Old Elsie, but Mam was there. She was too busy to pay me any attention; she was mixing a tonic like she'd said. The far wall was thick with long growths of dark, red-brown moss and in the corner a wide fissure ran from the floor to the ceiling. Mam was standing by the wall, leaning deep into the gap, her hands flat against the stone on each side. She was whispering her recipe into the darkness.

I stopped at the foot of the stairs, holding the rail, tense in case I needed to make a hasty retreat. I could hear Mam saying the same indistinct phrases over and over. They were the usual things. Something about the wound on Lee's arm. Something about him needing to forget. To sleep, to start again.

Beside her, a short spout grew from the moss at a slight downward angle. It looked a little like the root of a tree had forced its way through the wall, but it was pale and puce coloured, glinting with a natural moisture. Mam had set a glass beneath it on a wooden table. The tonic was slow coming; a thick, dark green-black liquid, it curled out of the spout on the wall and settled slowly, filling the bottom of the beaker.

"Mam," I said.

She flapped a hand to silence me. I waited, impatient, searching the shadows for any sign Old Elsie might already be there. Mam kept close to the crevice, and the thin threads of reddish moss that furred the stone walls wavered like river weeds in a current. They reached out to her gently. They brushed against her, cupping the shape of her face, curling around the back of her head, knitting and unknitting themselves. She kept talking, and the longer she spoke the more the tonic kept coming, until a low hiss sounded from the spout, signalling it was done. The pipe convulsed a little, then puckered closed.

Mam stopped talking and stepped back. As she did so, the tendrils of moss contracted away from her. She picked up the beaker and wiped the spout clean with a cloth.

I couldn't wait any longer.

"Old Elsie followed Lee home," I said. "She came up through his basement—"

"Robbie," Mam said, but when she turned to me, she looked through me. "Lee," she said.

I hadn't heard him follow me. I don't know what made me think he wouldn't, maybe it just didn't occur to me that I should care. But there he was, only a few steps away up the staircase, staring at Mam, his jaw hanging open in dumb surprise.

"Lee," Mam said again.

But Lee was shaking his head; he was backing up the staircase away from us.

"Lee," Mam said, but Lee was through the door. "Rob, stop him."

I didn't know what was going on, but I ran back up the stairs, shouting Lee's name.

As I stepped back into the hall, something leapt at me from behind the door. Something solid slammed into the side of my head and sent me sprawling across the carpet. My vision blurred, focussing only when Lee's Doc Martens landed in front of me. So close, they looked bright and scarred, the thick rubber of their soles glistening with viscous mud and broken leaf-mould. I looked up through a knot of pain to see Lee nursing a clenched hand. He was shaking his head as though he couldn't believe anything he had seen. His eyes had gone wild again, his breathing shallow.

"Bunch of freaks," he said, his voice tight, like someone holding back tears.

He glanced at the staircase to the basement, then booted me clean in the ribs, a short, sharp bolt of pain that made me see fireworks. And then he was away. And then he was gone, the door banging shut behind him.

3

We all grow up in different worlds. It can disorient us when we finally come to appreciate how our situation is unique. Having lived outside The Crescent for so long, I can now appreciate how odd it must sound, but I speak with absolute honesty when I say it was only much later that it made sense to me why Lee fled that night.

As far as I knew, there was a dispensary in the basement of all the houses in The Crescent. There must have been one in Number 21 as well, unless the Thorel brothers had blocked it up when they'd been sent in to clear the place before Lee and his da moved in. Maybe Lee's da had never been shown what it was. Maybe he just didn't want to know. Even that didn't strike me as far-fetched: for better or worse, it was usually the women who lived in The Crescent who were capable of using it properly after all. Da could never get it to do anything for him, he just shouted into the hole and the hole ignored him. It had something to do with the way Mr Olhouser made things work that I never really understood. Mam said he needed perspective, context and empathy, and Da was better at dealing with things in the moment rather than understanding how they fitted together. I was never entirely sure how much of this was true and how much of it was her being diplomatic.

Whenever one of us took ill or whenever one of us got hurt, our mam would tell it to the wall in the dispensary and in that way, she'd brew a tonic to keep us well. And those tonics kept us healthy, kept us strong. They kept us going for years and more, long past when anyone else would have stopped, given up, retired. Because that was how The Crescent worked. We took care of the city, we took care of Mr Olhouser, and he took care of us.

And so, as I lay curled on the carpet, as the door slammed shut behind Lee, I didn't understand why Lee had reacted as he had. I didn't understand what had made him run from the house. I wondered if what everyone had said about him was true after all. He was unstable, psychotic, prone to acts of violence, triggered by the smallest whim.

It is only with the unsparing clarity of hindsight that I appreciate how we each believed we had been betrayed by the other.

Mam had got me to bed by the time Da got home. She'd fed me a tonic of my own, bright red with the taste and texture I'd imagine of uncooked offal. Inside of me, any damage done by Lee's knuckles and boot was repaired under its influence, but the tonic couldn't heal everything. It couldn't allay the doubts that Lee's behaviour had seeded in me and so sleep did not come easy that night. I lay awake in my room, the sky gradually lightening outside, listening to the raised voices from the floor below.

Come the morning, I woke to find Mam sitting on the chair by my bed. She'd set a fresh glass of tonic on the cabinet. She told me I should stay in bed, and she reached across to feel my forehead, as though either of us believed I might have a temperature. I protested the curfew, but only lightly. I didn't really want to be there to witness the day drag by; it might be beautiful and sunny and full of wonderful things, but it could only be corrupted by the heavy weight of what had gone before.

Mam took my hand and when she smiled it looked like a compromise.

"I'd been in The Crescent only a few years when you were born," she said. "You've been here nearly as long as I have. Funny to think isn't it? The only reason they accept me here is because of you. Not your father, but you."

"That's not true, Mam."

She didn't meet my eyes, but frowned with concentration as though she was trying to remember things exactly.

"You got sick one day," she said. "You were so small, and your Da was on shift and I was all on my own with you and you were crying and crying and I didn't know what to do.

"And I was so scared. I really was, because I didn't know anyone here. I'd been here for a few years, but I was shy. The place frightened me because I never felt like I belonged. I was from the outside and even if no-one said anything, I knew they were thinking it. I tried to call the doctors but the phones were up and down. They never got anything fixed round here in those days. There'd be noise on the line that sounded like a train coming down a long tunnel, there was the endless sound of the engines beneath us that I still hadn't got used to..."

From somewhere outside, I could hear the siren indicating a change of shift at The Works. It felt earlier than I had been expecting, but Mam was still talking and I didn't want to look at my bedside clock to check what time it was.

"I'd never used the dispensary before," she said. "I didn't like it. I didn't like the basement at all. I always felt like I was being watched down there. But you were crying. You should have heard yourself. You were crying like the world was all on fire. Your face was like that of a little old man, red as a beetroot, and you were screaming to the heavens. So I carried you downstairs and I put aside everything that scared me about the place and I asked for help."

She turned to the window, and hesitated for long enough that I wondered if she had it in her to say anything else. But I felt her grip tighten around my hand.

"And there are days when I wish I never had," she said. "There are days when I wish I'd never gone down there, but instead taken you up in my arms and walked as far as I could until I found someone who could have told me what to do. There are days I wish I just kept walking, walking, walking..."

She pushed herself to her feet. I tried to piece together what she'd been saying.

"You'd have left Da?" I said.

She shook her head. "No," she said. "No, of course not."

But she stopped in the doorway, arrested by a thought. When she spoke again she didn't turn back to me.

"Sometimes you just do anything to try and belong," she said. "Like one of your grandmother's jigsaws. You take out a knife and cut off the parts that don't fit. It'll never be comfortable, it'll never really match whatever's around it, but sometimes it's just so much easier to make do."

She looked back and while she smiled I saw her eyes were rimmed with pink.

"Drink your tonic," she said. "It's good for you. And try and rest. I'll bring up your dinner on a tray."

I did what I was told, and as a consequence I missed everything that was going on outside during the day. I just lay back and let time fall away from me. I think I dreamed, but I don't remember anything other than a long, lingering blackness. The tonic does that sometimes.

By the time I finally got up, the sun was edging down the sky, folding up the day into red and orange stripes. I felt a bit unsteady on my feet, as if I'd been in bed longer than I really had.

I pulled on my clothes from the previous day and made my way downstairs, gingerly anticipating aches that didn't come.

There were voices in the kitchen, adult voices, low and serious; frighteningly calm. I hesitated in the hallway outside, reluctant to engage with them, but sometimes being quiet can draw its own attention and it felt as though my own silence had seeped ahead and announced me like a shadow. Mam stepped out and saw me at the foot of the stairs. She cooed over me first. She made me lift up my T-shirt so she could see how the bruises had healed.

"Craig's mam is here," she said. She gave a little half-smile that was only half-reassuring. "She just wants to ask you what happened."

I followed her into the kitchen, and saw Mrs Peveril was sitting at the kitchen table in the same place where Lee had sat the night before. There was a cup of tea in front of her and her hand was placed on the woodwork beside it, the clean, well-scrubbed spot where Lee's blood had pooled.

Da was still dressed in his overalls. He leaned against the back wall like it was as far away from her as he could get without leaving the room.

"Well," Mrs Peveril said, gesturing for me to take the chair opposite her. "I'd heard that this young man had been in the wars but he looks all right and proper to me."

She beamed. It was a well-practiced expression, but one that had never really suited her. She was quite a big woman. Not overweight, but both tall and square. She looked at me closely, and in contrast to the warmth promised by her wide smile her eyes were sharp little points that could have scored burning marks as she looked me up and down.

"He asked after you," she said, her smile shrinking to a point. "Mr Olhouser. He does worry. He's like a parent in that way. He worries a great deal."

She stirred her tea, absently.

Mam cleared her throat, I sensed her move behind me, I felt her hands on my shoulders.

"Marsha," Mam said. "He should rest. Robbie, you should go back to your bed."

"Nonsense," Mrs Peveril said. "He looks very rested. Your mother has such a gift in the dispensary. She knows exactly what to say to the old man. I know a few round here who could learn a thing or two from her."

She smiled widely and the expression looked like it had been crowbarred into position; it bunched up her face and shrank her eyes to slits.

"Let him stand on his own, Laura dear," she said, her tone cool but firm.

I felt Mam's hands let go of me. She stepped away to join Da, who was looking at the floor, breathing slow and regular.

"Robbie," Mrs Peveril said. "I want you to tell me why Lee Wrexler came here last night."

I took a long breath before answering her.

"He was scared," I said. I glanced to Mam to see if I was saying the right thing.

"There aren't any wrong answers, Robbie," Mrs Peveril said. "You haven't done anything bad. I just want you to tell me what you think happened last night."

A trace of movement made me look at my parents again. I saw Da's hand had found Mam's. He held it tightly and I wished one of them would take my hand as well. I wanted us to be all joined together. I didn't want to be left alone, unmoored in the room while Mrs Peveril was circling.

"He was scared," I said again.

"What was he scared of?"

"Old Elsie," I said. "He followed her. And then she followed him—"

Mrs Peveril laughed. A short, abrupt little laugh.

"Old Elsie?" she said. "What a thing to be scared of."

But like the smile, her laughter sounded forced. It was an artificial tone she might have used to address a child. And there was something about the way she kept checking over my shoulder to gauge my parents' reactions which made me appreciate there was something bigger going on. Something I hadn't been told.

"What happened?" I said.

"After he left your house last night," Mrs Peveril said, "your friend tried to set a fire, did you know that?"

"No!" My denial came out in such a rush Mrs Peveril's eyes narrowed.

"He didn't tell you what he was going to do?"

"He didn't say anything."

Mrs Peveril hadn't finished.

"This is what he did," she said. "He took the curtains from his father's house, he ripped them off their rails, all of them. And then he carried them across the green and lay them down at the door of another house in The Crescent. Then he covered them in lighter fluid and he lit a match."

I felt breathless, sick. I felt as though all the bruises Lee had inflicted on me were blossoming across my stomach and chest like dark crimson roses. A dull, nagging ache climbed up my chest to my throat.

"Where?" I said.

"Number 17," Mrs Peveril said. "Mr Olhouser's place."

I stumbled to my feet. I don't know what I'd been intending. To run to the door to see? To run to the bathroom and throw up? But I didn't get far before Da's arm caught me, wrapped around me. He felt warm. His overalls smelt of iron and oil and earth.

"It's alright, lad." He sounded gruff, tense, tired.

"Mr Olhouser's place doesn't simply burn down," Mrs Peveril said, as though that had been my concern.

"Where's Lee?"

"He's safe," she said, but the last syllable trailed like it could have been a question. She stood, pushing her chair back and smoothing her skirt.

"Mr Olhouser wants to see Lee," she said.

Mam looked horribly pale.

"Marsha," she said. "He's just a boy."

"Mr Olhouser has been very patient. Rest assured, he appreciates what you tried to do, but in light of more recent events, he has decided the boy represents a danger to The Crescent. Arson is arson, and that's not all. The boy's history is eye-opening, Laura. Did you hear what he did to his poor mother? And he's violent. You saw what he did to your boy and that was before he attempted to murder Mr Olhouser while he slept last night."

She smiled at us all.

"That sort of thing can't stand," she said. "He's a bad influence, a bad apple. And so therefore, this evening, there will be a lesson. The residents have been told. A detail from The Works will be on hand to supervise."

"Marsha…" Mam stepped forward as though she could put herself between her and me. "He tried to do something terrible, but he didn't. Not in the end. This is too much. Surely this is too much. He's just a boy."

"What if he had succeeded, Laura?" Mrs Peveril said. "That's not an outcome anyone should wish to consider."

"But, Marsha—"

"Laura, dear," Mrs Peveril said. "This has already been decided. As has this: your boy will witness."

I felt Da's arm tighten around me.

"No," he said.

Mrs Peveril turned her attention to him and I felt him wither under her scrutiny.

"Either he sees it with us, or he sees it alone," she said. "And if he sees it alone, I have no way of guaranteeing what lesson he'll be taught."

Mam stepped forward. "Marsha, there's no precedent—"

Mrs Peveril snapped around to stare at her.

"There's every precedent, Laura," she said. "And if you weren't from the outside yourself, you wouldn't say such foolish things. If I have reason to believe that The Crescent is under threat in any way – in any way – I will act accordingly. The two boys were friends and while I'm sure your son was led astray by the Wrexler lad, Mr Olhouser wants to be certain he understands."

She raised a warning finger.

"This isn't just about The Crescent. This isn't just about us. This is about the health of the city as a whole, you know that. Lessons are important and it's been too long since we've had one in this community. Given the events of recent days, it could be said the standards we once held in high regard have been slipping."

She looked at me, eyes sparkling over the rims of her glasses.

"And besides," she said. "He's a boy. From my experience, he may even enjoy it."

※

We left the house in an awkward procession. Mrs Peveril with her hand on my shoulder, Mam and Da a step or two behind. Floodlights borrowed from The Works had been set up on all sides, hooked to purring generators. Together, they lit up the green like a stadium and made the grass uncannily vivid. The Crescent had no need to hide its business from the world. The world had no business to look.

The whole of The Crescent were there, and they were an organised crowd. Most of the men from The Works lined up along the periphery of the green, forming a human wall. The women were inside, gathered in a tight huddle around Number 17. The kids had been bundled into supervised smaller groups, arranged across the street, behind the row of men. They craned their heads for a better view.

Everyone had turned towards us, watching with a queasy sense of expectancy that Mrs Peveril appeared to relish. She let go of me and walked ahead of us, leading us onward like a proud mother duck. She walked tall and the attention made her taller.

The kids around the pavement watched us solemnly. I searched them for sympathetic faces, but I could only find Lisa's and it was as stiff as a mask.

The line of men split to allow us to pass through them. I felt Da touch my hand, and then he broke away from our group and hung back, folding into the men's ranks, reforming behind us, sealing us inside.

As we neared Number 17, I saw Lee was there. He was being held upright between the Thorel brothers but he hung limp and spent. His jacket was gone and his T-shirt looked torn.

It looked as though the fight in him had gone already and that alone felt wrong to me. The Lee I imagined I knew would not have given up so soon. That Lee would still be fighting, he'd be a whirling ball of energy, all knees and elbows and flailing fists and feet. Even if they could keep him in check, the Thorels would be busy with him; they'd have lost teeth by now, they'd be black and blue. But the real Lee looked exhausted and the Thorels held him loosely between them. He was just a kid after all.

He lifted his head as he saw me coming and when his eyes met mine it was as though the ground had softened under my feet and I stumbled, winded by the look of him. He didn't look angry with me. He didn't look like he would forgive me if he had the chance. He didn't even look scared anymore. He simply looked blank and tired, like he was done fighting and wanted everything to be over.

It occurred to me then that the only person I hadn't seen was Lee's da. I craned around to scan the line of men on the far side of the green, but the light of the floods only highlighted the strips of reflective material around the seams of their overalls, making them a paperchain of stick men in the dark. Was Lee's da amongst them? What could he have been told that would make him just stand there impassively, watching with everyone else?

I felt Mam take my hand; she held it tight and we watched Mrs Peveril approach Lee. She stopped before him and I could see her stooping slightly to say something to him. He stared at her with hangdog eyes and she straightened, stepping past him to the door. She knocked twice, then turned around and looked at me pointedly.

The command in her expression was unmistakable, but I lingered stubbornly until I felt Mam nudge me forward.

"It'll be alright," she said, her voice barely raised above a whisper. It struck me at the time as such a strange thing to say. It was a reassurance given but not fully believed, the sort of promise which might be given to a kid before a sticky plaster was ripped clean from a wound on their arm.

As we reached the small gate to the patch of garden in front of Number 17, I felt Mam let go of me, and without her there was a coldness in the air which hadn't troubled me before. I turned to see her being led back to the group of women waiting around the garden gate. I recognised Mrs Bolam, the twins' mother, and Mrs Clay from next door. They gathered Mam amongst them, and by the way their concern reflected her own I saw she was not an outsider to them in the way that Mrs Peveril believed. But her eyes were wide and brimming; the light made them glitter like beads of shattered glass.

Behind me, Lee said my name and I turned to face him.

It was just the three of us in the little front garden of Number 17. Mrs Peveril, Lee and me. The Thorel brothers were there too, but they were like great lumps of wood; they were barely there at all.

Lee looked at me and his expression was all over the place. His eyes were wild and flickering like they couldn't quite focus anymore.

"I'm sorry," I said.

The words came out broken, but maybe he heard. A slow smile inched across his face and he opened his mouth, wetting his lips as though to reply.

But before he could do so, the door to Number 17 opened. It swung silent and unattended, and with little more to show for himself than a brisk coolness in the air, Mr Olhouser invited us inside.

The houses in The Crescent were almost all the same. They were bland and grey and semi-detached. Built sometime in the thirties, the layout of each was reflected along the adjoining wall with its neighbour. So in a sense, Number 17 was the same as the house I lived in. There was the same hallway, the same stairs, the same lounge to the right of the front door, the same kitchen to the back.

Only this house was empty. There didn't seem to be any power, so a series of work lights had been set up leading down the hallway, connected by a spaghetti tangle of yellow and black cables. While the walls were bright, the shadows pooled in the folds between them and I remember there was still a faint chemical smell, as though the rooms had been freshly painted. The floorboards were polished and the woodwork was crisp but there was no furniture, no light fittings, no pictures on the walls. The door on the right led to the equivalent of the lounge in our house, but here the door gaped, showing nothing but dark geometries of a neglected space, washed a gloomy colour by the halogen lights from the green outside.

With a brisk and familiar confidence, Mrs Peveril led us past the foot of the staircase to the room at the back of the house where the door stood closed. Here, she stopped and hesitated just long enough to make me doubt the sum of her confidence.

She knocked. "Mr Olhouser," she said, her voice adopting a singsong cadence as though she were playing hide and seek with a child.

She glanced back at us and smiled sweetly. I could hear Lee's breathing, quick and uneven.

If she received a reply, I didn't hear it, but Mrs Peveril opened the door anyway and pushed it wide. In our house, the back room was the kitchen, but here it was empty. Unlike the other rooms we'd passed, the floor was fitted with a thick, rich, amber carpet that even then struck me as incongruous. It was bright and cheerful and quite at odds with the otherwise monochrome blankness of the empty house. As the door opened, the dense warmth of the room leaked out into the hall, bringing with it a musty smell of compost and over-boiled vegetables.

I had become used to the noise of The Works. That deep bass rumble, that rhythmic thud, thud, thud. It was familiar enough to me that I may not have been paying attention to it when we first stepped into the house, but when Mrs Peveril opened the door to the kitchen, I did notice how the sound which had been with me all of my life seemed to get louder, as though I was now closer to its source than ever before. It sounded clearer, too, and for the first time it occurred to me that the sound I had always assumed to be machines working deep under the ground no longer sounded like metal gears or engines. It sounded like rocks grinding over each other, water running freely, the distant, distinct thud of a heartbeat quickening in anticipation.

I had a strong sense there was someone inside the room, watching us standing there in the doorway, but I couldn't see anyone, only our own reflections in the black glass of the windows overlooking the garden.

"Lee," Mrs Peveril said.

Lee was staring at the windows, his face drained. He shook his head and tried to step backwards. He'd been there before of course, on the other side of those forbidding black panes of glass. Even though I hadn't shared his experience I understood his fear all too well, because there was something about that room that made me desperate to be somewhere else. There was something about the way the darkness gathered in it, something about the warmth of it, the smell of it, that made it feel comprehensively wrong. I couldn't be certain, but the bright, thick carpet seemed to harbour a faint luminescence of its own that gave the room the dull, artificial glow of an electric fireplace.

Overall, it was a feeling of claustrophobia, as though the walls were slowly shrinking inwards, as though the air was becoming heavier and more humid. I could feel the atmosphere of the place clawing at my lungs, reaching deeper inside of me. I thought of Lee's story, those tree stumps he'd described in the garden, and even though the windows showed nothing but darkness their proximity was enough that my only thought was escape.

"Forward, Lee." Mrs Peveril's smile was fixed.

"No," said Lee.

"It would be rude to keep Mr Olhouser waiting."

"There's no-one there." Lee leaned forward a little, squinting into the dark.

"Mr Olhouser?" Mrs Peveril glanced through the door as though he might be there, listening to her. "Who do you think Mr Olhouser is, Lee?"

Lee stared at her, confused.

"Some guy," he said. "Thinks he runs the city."

Mrs Peveril shook her head.

"Stupid child," she said. "Mr Olhouser *is* the city."

She'd barely spoken when Mick Thorel stepped up behind Lee and shoved him roughly, his big hand flat in the small of Lee's back, moved with the force of a pile driver. I remember how it seemed like such childish behaviour at the time. There was no strategy behind it, just brute petulance. But that was all it took. Lee fell forward, arms windmilling. He danced to stay upright, one step, two steps and he was over the threshold and inside the room before he could even think about what he was doing.

From somewhere deep beneath us, there was the sound of a long held breath being expelled with a weary inevitability. Lee twisted around, and looked up to meet my eyes. He didn't have time to say anything. A shadow passed, the door swung closed with a whisper. And he was gone.

I didn't see what happened to Lee, but god help me I heard it all.

Lee's voice sounded such a long way away. It sounded so small I couldn't make out any words, I can't even be sure if there were any.

Around him, that deep roaring resonance built to a muffled roar, and with it I heard a chorus of busy clicks and taps and pops. There was a sound like fingernails on glass.

Then, for a moment, everything stopped, and in a way the silence felt worse because for some reason I understood it couldn't last. It didn't; there was a dull cracking sound like a green branch being snapped with deliberation, and with it a wail so sudden and raw it sounded more animal than human.

And then there was a louder sound, so close to the other side of the door it made me recoil from it. A wet, flapping noise: snapping and creaking, painfully unhurried, like something dragging its own weight with agonising slowness. With it came the smell of long-standing water, of vegetation turned to rot, and even with a door between us the heat in the air thickened and I felt perspiration prickling across my skin.

Mrs Peveril reached for my arm.

"Rob," she said.

I started at her touch, completely forgetting I wasn't alone. My face was burning with tears. I did not even know I had been crying.

"Robert," Mrs Peveril said, her voice soft. "You can make it easier for him if you choose." She glanced behind me to where Mick Thorel stood.

He nodded in acknowledgement and reached into the back pocket of his overalls. He produced a baton, a cosh, and he held it out for me to take. Dull grey like a roll of lead, it was scarred and battered along its half-metre length. Mick's big face was impassive, his eyes were dead. But I saw a thin trail of sweat inch its way down the side of his jaw.

Mrs Peveril moved forward and put her hand on the door.

Mick didn't move, his hand outstretched, and so, dumbly, I took the cosh from him. It felt heavy in my hand; it felt solid, cold to the touch and horribly real.

Mrs Peveril turned the handle, and without taking her eyes from me, she started to push the door open.

For some reason, I thought it would be locked. The way the door had closed was so firm and decisive I imagined it was never meant to be opened again. But it gave easily at her touch, and a thin seam of darkness widened along its edge.

And it was dark. A suffocating, unsparing dark. The smell of rot intensified, the heat swelled as the door opened wider and a horrible curiosity overtook me. For a moment, just a moment, I think I would have given anything to have seen whatever it was that Lee saw, just so I would have *known*, just so I'd have understood. And as the door opened wider, I felt myself leaning closer, squinting at the blackness.

A little more, I thought, and I'll see. Just a little more. Just a tiny bit more.

Mrs Peveril smiled. I sensed Mick Thorel shift behind me and the spell shattered into panic.

I dropped the cosh, and without sparing a final glance at the widening doorway, I fled.

Down the hall, past the foot of the stairs, past the empty lounge. Around me, the shadows of the house seemed to rush together as though they were racing me. There was the sound of something moving, scuttling on the dark staircase behind me, but I didn't look back. As I reached the front door and wrenched it open, I heard Mrs Peveril behind me. She spoke sharply.

"Let him go," she said.

I still don't know who it was she was talking to.

✤

I emerged, blinking into the brightness of the floodlit green, and Mam broke away from the other women to meet me at the garden gate. She enveloped me in a hug and I sobbed into her chest. She held me tight, she felt so warm, so alive.

She steered me away from the house and I let her lead me through the waiting crowd. I had a vague sense of the people around us, a sense of them parting, letting us through.

"Where is he?" It was a raised voice: anger and bravado trimmed with fear. It carried above the hushed murmur of the crowd like something sharp and broken that didn't belong. Lee's da was running across the green. He ran with a slight limp, and as he came closer I saw his face was masked with bruises and lacerations; his eyes were red and raw.

"What have you done with my son?"

He didn't see me as he ran to where Mrs Peveril and the Thorel brothers were standing by the front gate of Number 17.

"Where is he?" Quieter this time. "Let me through."

"Mr Olhouser has no wish to see you at this time," Mrs Peveril said.

"Fuck him. Let me through."

"No."

"Let me through," he said. "You can't do this."

He marched towards the house, but the crowd of women from The Crescent swelled in front of him, blocking his way. A sea of impassive faces, bright under the floodlights. He faltered, his resolve fraying.

"You can't do this," he said again, speaking to the crowd in a low murmur. He turned back to Mrs Peveril. "I'll call the police."

Mrs Peveril stood straight and unmoved.

"Without The Crescent," she said, "there would be no city. Without the city, there would be no police. Call them. They will listen. They will sympathise, but they won't come. Communities like ours have existed long before the cities that grew out of them. We are older than law. They know that."

Lee's da just stood there for a moment, his head hung limp. Then he turned around swiftly and lunged at Mrs Peveril. Mick Thorel anticipated him and stepped smartly into his path. As Lee's da lurched close, Mick took a swing at him and there was a dull crack as his solid-oak knuckles connected with something softer. Lee's da tumbled, sprawling inelegantly on the grass.

I took an involuntary step towards the scene, a sense of impotent responsibility driving my muscles, determined to make some gesture, no matter how small, but I felt Mam's arm tense around me, and I let her hold me back, giving in too easily to another's concern.

Lee's da struggled to his feet. He looked winded, and as his face glittered under the lights I wondered if there were tears there. When he spoke again, his voice sounded as though it had been broken and too-hastily repaired.

"Let me see him," he said. "Please."

"I'm sorry." Mrs Peveril shook her head.

"He's all I've got."

"I'm sorry."

"You can't do this."

"It's done."

Lee's da fell to his knees in front of Mrs Peveril. He snatched at her hand and when she discretely moved it away from him I saw his body convulse, as though he was fighting for breath.

"Please," he said. His voice was barely a whisper, but it carried across the green like a prayer.

Mrs Peveril looked first startled, then amused. She stooped down and spoke to him quietly. She glanced up at where Mam and I stood, then she turned away and left the man kneeling alone in the mud.

One by one, the crowd began to disperse. Slowly, silently, they drifted away until Lee's da was alone on the green.

Humiliated, he pushed himself to his feet. A sad and solitary figure, he was hangdog in posture, but there was a wiry strength clenched within him still. He turned to look directly at me as though he knew I'd been there from the start.

"He was your friend," he said. His voice wasn't loud, but its aim was unwavering, it struck me clean and cut through me. Even with the distance between us, I could see how shadows now outlined his features. There was grief there, there was an aching loss, and as if blessed by some sudden, horrible premonition, I could see how they would not soften and fade, but how they would harden and sharpen instead.

"You were supposed to be his friend." His voice was louder and there was a rawness to it that splintered the edges.

I so wanted to say something in return. I wanted to say something that might help, something that might heal. I wanted to answer him in the way he deserved, but language had abandoned me and I just stood there, mouth agape, waiting passively for the right words to find me.

"He was your friend." His voice was shriller and he took a step towards us.

Mam tugged at my arm.

"Come home," she said.

For the second time that evening, I turned away. I let myself be led home. And far behind us, alone on the green, Lee's da was screaming.

4

The weekend after my birthday that year, Da took me fishing out at the Hollow. It was a dull grey day, and there weren't any boats out, but we sat by the water and waited, wrapped up warm, me in my winter coat, Da in his donkey jacket.

Da and I had been fishing together often enough to know you don't need to say anything to each other while you're doing it. We were there for nearly an hour before he spoke to me.

"When you get older," he said, "you turn your back on this place and you never look back."

He stared out across the water. He was wearing his work boots. Pressed deep into the loam, black, spiralling water pooled around the rubber soles.

I protested, saying the things I thought I should say to prove myself loyal. My friends were here, my family.

Everything I knew was in The Crescent, and it was all true: I knew nothing about the world outside, and in some way it frightened me more.

His face was set.

"When you get older," he said again, "you turn your back on this place and you never look back."

It took a few more years, but I did as I was told. I knuckled down at school and scraped through with grades enough to get by. Ultimately, it became the only thing I could do. After the lesson on the green, Lisa and Nancy and Sid turned their back on me. That was what they had been taught that day; that I'd been too close to Lee. Close enough I was treated as though some unquantifiable outsiderness had rubbed off and left me corrupt.

I never talked to them about what I'd seen in Number 17, I never told anyone how my own house seemed different now its shape and dimensions matched Mr Olhouser's place. I never told anyone how the kitchen with its big windows no longer seemed safe to me, to the extent that I would hesitate too long on its threshold whenever I was meant to go in, or how I would hurry past the door to the basement, or look at the darkened staircase as though something might be there, waiting for me.

I never told anyone how I would remember Lee's face, moon-bright with horror as the door closed. For a while, I thought that was all I saw, but somewhere deep in the periphery there were fragments that lodged deep in my memory, assembling themselves only later, when I revisited the scene alone in my room, waking drenched in sweat, my bedside light still burning away the dark.

There would be Lee as he always was, framed by the narrowing doorway. And as he turned to look at me, I saw the carpet under his feet convulse. Its long mossy threads stretching and wavering in hungry, rippling currents like the fronds of an anemone in a sheltered tide.

Every time, before the door closed, I would wake in my bed, in the room that had always been familiar to me. But in that moment, shocked out of the dream, my room in The Crescent had never felt so alien and exposed. I would be left with the unshakable sense that I had woken just a moment too late to see towering shapes coagulating in the shadows around me.

When I was sixteen, I left The Crescent. I haven't been back since.

I still keep in touch with my parents, but I rarely see them. They're cautious. My da doesn't like me phoning them because he doesn't trust anyone not to be listening. I write them letters instead; I send them to a place in town where Mam picks them up. It's like something out of one of Da's spy novels and I suspect the subterfuge is distraction enough to give him some degree of comfort. On rare occasions we meet up out of town. Da borrows a car and makes some big excuse I can't imagine anyone really falling for.

They pass on the news they have. Craig married Lisa and everyone pretended it was a surprise. They told me how all the houses were covered in brightly coloured bunting, and how there was a bonfire in the middle of the green and how there was dancing through the night until late the following day. Sid Parry got married too, but his was lower key. He met a girl from the estate, and they've moved into Sid's uncle's place at Number 3. They're talking about kids. Everyone's talking about them having kids.

Lee's da's still there, they tell me. He doesn't say anything these days, but he works harder than anyone. Da says he's still waiting for Olhouser to meet with him; Mam says Da talks rubbish and worse.

They look older than I feel they should do, like they're living their lives on fast-forward without me. Sometimes I wonder if whatever tonic the Olhouser feeds them to keep them well is no longer as potent as it once was; sometimes I realise that they are old now, so maybe the tonic is keeping them going longer than they deserve. When we part, I watch them walking away from me, hunched together, the one reaching out blindly for the other and it feels so wrong to me that we should have to part again, always so soon.

They do all of this because they think it'll protect me. After all these years, they think it'll keep me and Mr Olhouser apart. But I don't think it works like that.

I find myself drawn to other cities. Each has its own crescent somewhere on the map; each has its own deep resonance which you can hear if you listen hard enough; each has its own Olhouser, or whatever name it chooses for itself. There are allegiances between towns I don't understand. Some are independent, some are benign, some are inattentive; you just have to look close to see.

Sometimes I see Old Elsie. Pushing through a crowd, her back curved and head bowed, those clusters of carrier bags held tight in each hand. I don't know how she travels from The Crescent, but she does. I've seen her in Glasgow, Boston, Lyon, Sydney. She's always standing still, I've never once seen her move. There are the others too. The Priest lingers on street corners, wavering and decrepit. I saw him on the corner of Westminster in London, where crowds of brokers on their morning commute split to pass round him unaware of his muttered benedictions, his palsied hands tracing crosses in the air. I've only seen Copper the once; he was directing pigeons in the square of a small town south of Burgos in Northern Spain. I swear he grinned as he saw me: all broken teeth and blackened tongue.

I haven't seen Lee, but I fear that one day I will. I don't even know if that's how things work, but there are days like this morning when I keep thinking he's there, waiting and watching in some hidden doorway. Or I imagine I'll see him standing motionless in a shifting crowd, staring out at me with someone else's eyes. I don't think there'll be judgment there. I don't think there'll be anything much anymore. I don't want to see Lee again, but sometimes I think that one day, I will need to.

I circle my own origin but never approach. Everything is transitory: places, lovers, work. Drink is a constant, drink and worry and shame. Sometimes I stare at my own reflection, listless and pale in a hostel washroom. There's not much left of The Crescent kid who used to scare his classmates or distract shop assistants from Lee's crimes. I look older, leaner, achingly tired. I still don't sleep well, but it's not because of the dreams. I miss the clank and pound and grind of The Works, I desperately miss the sound of the engines beneath me, forever turning somewhere deep in the earth. The silence of other places nags at me in the dark. I block my ears so I can hear the current of my own blood pounding in my ears, but it isn't the same. It isn't the same at all.

I'm slowly hunching into myself as I block myself away from the world, and sometimes, when I see the grey bags under my eyes, I wonder if that's how it begins. If the next morning my body will wake up without me and pick its way home.

And I think of my parents. And I think of the friends who were so quick to forget me. And I think of those long hot summers stretched out on the green. Sometimes I think back to that time when the Thorel brothers took down the shutters from Number 21, before Lee and his da moved into The Crescent. The colony of mice, grown content they understood the scale of the world they'd been born into. But they were blind to its context until the walls had been so rudely ripped away. And I wonder if given the choice, they would have settled for ignorance in exchange for a world they could comprehend.

I used to think I still saw Elsie and the others because when Olhouser was bored with toying with me, they would step forward from the shadows and drag me away with them, back through their secret paths to the red-carpeted room at Number 17.

But as the years have passed, I don't think that's true anymore. I remember the way Lee's da stared at me on the green that night and now I think I understand what he saw. He saw what Old Elsie, The Priest and the others see. They know what I am. They know where I belong. They know I want to go back, even though right now I won't admit it to myself. They know how The Crescent looks after its own.

And one day, when I've had enough of pretending I'm something I'm not, one day when I'm ready, like a tired old dog who's simply had enough, they'll be there to lead me home.

ACKNOWLEDGEMENTS

Thank you Andy Cox, Helena Bell, Usman Malik, Helen Marshall, Kelly Sandoval, Allison Solano and everyone from CW13.

ABOUT THE AUTHOR

Malcolm Devlin's stories have appeared in *Black Static*, *Interzone*, *Nightscript*, and *Shadows And Tall Trees*. His collection, *You Will Grow Into Them*, is published by Unsung Stories.

TTA NOVELLAS

1: Eyepennies by Mike O'Driscoll (sold out)
2: Spin by Nina Allan (sold out)
3: Cold Turkey by Carole Johnstone (sold out)
4: The Teardrop Method by Simon Avery
5: Engines Beneath Us by Malcolm Devlin
6: Honeybones by Georgina Bruce (out now)

Available from shop.ttapress.com

ALSO BY TTA PRESS

Interzone: bimonthly magazine of science fiction & fantasy
Black Static: bimonthly magazine of new horror fiction
Crimewave: occasional anthology of new crime fiction

Issues and subscriptions available from shop.ttapress.com